First published in Dutch as
Verdwaald in de Sneeuw
© 2002 Uitgeverij Clavis, Amsterdam – Hasselt
English version © 2003 Floris Books, 15 Harrison Gardens, Edinburgh
Reprinted 2004
British Library CIP Data available
ISBN 0-86315-384-4
Printed in Italy

Renne

The Ice Horse

Floris Books

Far in the northern grasslands a little skewbald horse lived in a herd of wild Icelandic horses. The herd had many mares and foals and was guided by a lean, black stallion.

The little horse's mane and tail were so long that they nearly reached the ground. He ate the sweet rich grass and ran freely over the hills.

Icelandic Horses were brought to Iceland by the Vikings in the ninth century. They have long manes and long thick tails. They are hardy animals, which means that they can live outdoors in winter as well as in summer, as long as they have some shelter from the weather.

The summer was almost gone and the black stallion decided that it was time for the little horse to leave the herd.

The little horse didn't understand what was happening, but the black stallion was very strong. So the little skewbald horse sadly left his friends, but stayed close by.

Icelandic horses are sociable creatures which live in herds, and need social contact with other horses. Young stallions usually stay with the herd until they are about two or three years old, when they are driven out by the dominant stallion.

During the autumn the horses ate the tasty lush grass, but now winter started to close in and the weather became colder and colder.

"We must leave immediately for the winter grasslands," said the black stallion.

The little horse tried to follow the herd, but the black stallion chased him away.

"But I want to come with you," cried the little horse.

"Go away!" shouted the stallion. "You don't belong to the herd anymore."

The little horse was very confused. He followed the herd from a distance, but his friends soon disappeared.

The first snow started to fall thickly. The little horse cleared away the snow with his hoof to find some grass to eat. He was very lonely.

Icelandic Horses are herbivores and eat mostly grass. In the winter they also eat hay, and love the occasional carrot or apple. They need to drink lots of clean fresh water each day. A horse will die if it does not drink for two days.

The snow fell thickly and covered the land in a pure white blanket. The little skewbald horse wandered all alone through the snow until eventually he reached a huge cliff at the end of a valley.

The storm was getting worse and worse. And the snow was falling very heavily.

Suddenly through the whirling snowflakes the little horse found the entrance to a cave. He rushed inside, glad to be out of the freezing snow.

But in the warmth of the cave he started to think about his friends outside on the hillsides. What would become of them?

The little horse could not stay in his warm cave while his friends were freezing. He had to help them. With a last look at the warm cave he went back out into the storm to look for his friends.

He struggled against the deep snow, and battled with the raging winds. On and on he went until eventually he arrived at the winter grasslands, which were covered in snow and ice.

The Icelandic climate is very harsh in the winter. The horses have a very thick winter coat, so that when it rains the skin underneath does not get wet. When they are outdoors in a snowstorm the snow just lies on top of their backs.

Suddenly he saw the herd. They were standing like frozen statues, with the snow lying on their backs.

The little horse ran towards them.

Icelandic Horses learn from their mothers and older horses what to eat, how to find food in the winter and where to shelter in bad weather.

Suddenly the black stallion appeared and blocked his way.

"What do you want here?" he asked.

"You have to come with me. If you don't, you will all freeze. You must let me pass!" said the little horse.

"No!" said the black stallion and attacked with enormous power.

This time the little skewbald horse fought back. The lives of the other horses depended on him.

They battled for an hour, kicking, biting and rearing. Finally, the little horse proved stronger than the black stallion and chased him away. Then he led the mares and foals to the warmth and safety of the cave.

Stallions can fight ferociously to keep leadership over the mares. They kick, rear and try to bite each other. The winner eventually chases the loser away and gains control over the herd.

The horses sheltered in the warm cave waiting for the storm to die down. Suddenly a black shadow appeared in the entrance to the cave. It was the black stallion trying to escape the snow and ice.

He looked tired and very, very cold. The little horse decided to let him stay.

Soon the weather changed and spring returned. The little horse was now a fully-grown skewbald stallion and had become the leader of the herd.

As soon as the snow melted he led the mares and foals back to the summer grazing grounds to eat the rich sweet grass, and run freely over the hills.